PLAIN NOODLES

For Carla, Josh and Bonnie.
B.W.

For Laura.
J.F.

Text copyright © 1989 by Betty Waterton
Illustrations copyright © 1989 by Joanne Fitzgerald
First paperback printing 1990
Second printing 1994
All rights reserved. No part of this book may be
reproduced or transmitted in any form or by any
means without permission in writing from the
publisher, except by a reviewer, who may quote brief
passages in a review.

A Meadow Mouse Paperback
Groundwood Books
Douglas & McIntyre Ltd.
585 Bloor Street West
Toronto, Ontario M6G 1K5

Canadian Cataloguing in Publication Data

Waterton, Betty
Plain noodles

"A Meadowmouse paperback."
ISBN 0-88899-132-0

I. Fitzgerald, Joanne, 1956– . II. Title.

PS8595.A796P63 1990   jC813'.54   C90-095084-6
P27.W37P1 1990

Design by Michael Solomon
Printed and bound in Hong Kong by
Everbest Printing Co. Ltd.

PLAIN NOODLES

BY Betty Waterton

PICTURES BY Joanne Fitzgerald

**A Meadow Mouse
Paperback**
Groundwood/Douglas & McIntyre
Toronto/Vancouver

HEINEMANN · LONDON

ONE sunny day when it was neither spring nor summer, Captain Norm came whistling out of his lighthouse and nearly tripped over his wife. She was sitting on the top step, looking miserable. Now and then she moaned a little moan.

"What's the matter, Julia?" asked the Captain. "Have you got a stomach ache?"

"No," she sighed. "I'm just lonesome for babies. I miss our little bambinos so much!"

"But they aren't little bambinos any more. They're the Famous Flying Figgs, of the circus!" said the Captain. "Why don't you come fishing with me?" But his wife shook her head.

"If I could find a nice purple starfish with pink arms ... or maybe a pink starfish with purple arms ... I might go painting."

The Captain put on his lucky yellow gumboots and went out in his rowboat. Mrs. C put on her painting hat and walked down to the beach.

There was an interesting-looking starfish stuck to a big rock, so she began to paint. But she had no sooner got one arm done when she heard a strange gurgling sound.

That doesn't sound like periwinkles, polliwogs or pigeons, she thought. *Nor even seagulls, seals or sea lions!*

She peeked around the rock — and got the surprise of her life.

There, bobbing gently in the water, was a little boat full of babies!

"It's a miracle!" she cried, as she waded into the shallow water, shoes and all, and pulled the dinghy onto the beach.

A small girl with orangey-red hair jumped out onto the sand. "Everybody out!" the girl called. "I'm Rosie and I'm three." She looked at Mrs. Grossman with eyes as green as the sea. "Do you have any breakfast?"

"No, but I have minestrone, ravioli, tortellini or plain noodles," replied Mrs. Figg, leading the way to the lighthouse.
"Plain noodles, please."

In the kitchen, everybody ate. Then they had milk out of Mrs. Figg's flowered cups.

"I need to go potty," Rosie said.

"Oh, my goodness," cried Mrs. Figg. "I'd forgotten all about things like that!" She pointed Rosie to the bathroom and rummaged in a trunk for some soft old flannelette diapers. "I knew these would come in handy someday," she said.

As she changed all the babies, she sang to them to keep them from squirming. After a while she ran out of diaper pins, so she used sticky tape. When she ran out of sticky tape, she sewed the diapers on.

The little ones ran off to play.

"I like it here. It's not boring," Rosie said, standing on her head and waving her legs in the air.

"Where did you come from?"

"A picnic. Our mothers all had a nap, but we weren't sleepy. So I found a little boat on the beach and we just sort of floated around the corner."

BOO-BAW! BOO-BAW! came a loud bellowing sound. Rosie fell off the sofa.

"Is that a dinosaur?" she wondered.
"It's the foghorn," said Mrs. Eigg. "But it's not supposed to do that when the sun is shining!" And she scurried up the winding stairs to the top of the lighthouse.

It was full of babies. They were lurching about, pushing buttons and twirling knobs. Lights flashed, the radio spluttered and the foghorn bellowed.

Mrs. Figg leaped here and there, scooping up babies and trying to turn things off. Then through the noise she heard a crash downstairs.

Shooing the babies before her, she ran down to the kitchen.

Rosie stood on a chair by the sink. "I'm doing the dishes," she said. There was no dishwasher.

Mrs. Figg skated across the slippery floor, sweeping up broken cups. After that, she mopped.

The babies were getting sleepy. Mrs. Figg carried them two by two into the bedroom, laid them in a row on the bed and tucked a soft blue blanket around them.

Sitting down in the squeaky rocking chair, she began to sing.

Twinkle, twinkle little starfish,
Sometimes pink and sometimes purplish...

Outside the sun shone brightly and the foghorn bellowed. BOO-BAW, BOO-BAW!

Meanwhile, out at sea, Captain ~~Figg~~ Norm rowed home for all he was worth. He had heard the foghorn and was coming to investigate.

The Captain landed on the island, raced through the kitchen and dashed up the winding stairs to his office. He pushed buttons and twirled knobs until finally the lights stopped flashing, the radio stopped spluttering and the foghorn stopped bellowing.

Then he heard another noise, but it was just his wife singing. He found her in the bedroom. On the bed, fast asleep, was a row of babies.

"Don't wake them," sang Mrs. Figg. "Or you'll be sorry!"

"I think I already am," said her husband. "Did you know there's somebody in the kitchen making noodles?"

"That's Rosie. She's very helpful. Still, I'd better go and see."

But as soon as Mrs. Figg stood up, the rocking chair stopped squeaking. The babies promptly woke up and started to cry.

Just then Rosie came in. She had noodles in her hair. She looked at the wailing babies and said, "They're probably wet again."

"But I don't have any more diapers," cried Mrs. Egg as she tried to shush the babies.

"Well, it doesn't matter,"
said Rosie. "Because I think our mothers are coming."

As they listened they heard a hubbub. It was the mothers clumping into the lighthouse. They swooped into the bedroom with whoops of joy and picked up their babies.

After they had left, the ~~Figgs~~ Crossmans stood on the steps of the ~~lake~~house waving goodbye.

"I guess you'll miss all those little bambinos," the Captain said to his wife.

"I won't have time," she replied. "Because they're going to have their picnics right here all summer!"

The Captain rubbed his stomach. "I'm really hungry! What's for supper, Julia?"

"Well, there's minestrone, ravioli, tortellini and plain noodles."

"That sounds good!" said the Captain.

"Do you mind helping yourself, dear?" said Mrs. C. "I've got to finish my starfish picture before the tide comes in."

And she put on her painting hat and went down to the beach.